MONSTER HIGH

SUMMER
SCARECATION

AN ACTIVITY JOURNAL
FOR GHOULS

Little, Brown and Company

Hachette Book Group
237 Park Avenue, New York, NY 10017
Visit our website at www.lb-kids.com

Little, Brown and Company is a division of Hachette Book Group, Inc.
The Little, Brown name and logo are trademarks of Hachette Book Group, Inc.

The publisher is not responsible for websites (or their content) that are not owned by the publisher.

First Edition: April 2013

Library of Congress Control Number: 2012955901

ISBN 978-0-316-24652-1

10 9 8 7 6 5 4 3

CW

Printed in the United States of America

MONSTER HIGH

SUMMER SCARECATION
AN ACTIVITY JOURNAL FOR GHOULS

Written by
Pollygeist Danescary

Little, Brown and Company
New York Boston

WELCOME TO SUMMER SCARECATION!

FUN MONSTER FREAK-OUTS AWAIT YOU!

School is out, and summer is in! This scarecation guide has the hottest tips and tricks for having a totally claw-some summer.

- Your friends from Monster High have travel tips. (Jetting to Scaris? Bring perfume! Going to Gloom Beach? Bring sunscream!)
- They have creeperific camping tips. (Dress to impress in your must-have pretty scary woodswear!)
- They have tips for making scareaway camp spooktacular, keeping family road trips from being a dead bore, using Uncreepable Code to keep in touch with your ghoulfriends, and having fangtastic fun all summer long!

Now it's time to get started, so turn the page, ghoulfriend. Scarecation is here!

Let's get amped up for a voltage summer!

It's of spooktacular importance to keep your ghoulfriend circuits open, so you can KIT until school starts again. You are going to have so many new things to talk about. You'll be going to new places, meeting new people, doing new things, and wearing scary-cute new clothes. So talking to your ghoulfriends will be more important than ever!

KIT

CONTACT INFO THAT YOU NEED:

Cell numbers to add to your iCoffin contacts

_____-_____-_____

_____-_____-_____

_____-_____-_____

Home numbers to reach your friends on their deadlines

_____-_____-_____

_____-_____-_____

_____-_____-_____

E-mail addresses to use for daily monster-mails

_____@_____.com

_____@_____.com

_____@_____.com

Scarecation addresses so you can write scale mail

_____
STREET
_____
CITY, STATE, ZIP

_____
STREET
_____
CITY, STATE, ZIP

_____
STREET
_____
CITY, STATE, ZIP

Do you need to write a top secret letter to protect a source? Use an Uncreepable Code to keep your message secure?

Starting with any letter except **A**, write out the entire alphabet, wrapping around to the beginning when you reach **Z**. Now write the numbers 1 through 26 below the letters. To write a secret message, replace each letter with the number it's paired with. Make sure your ghoulfriend knows the code, so she can decipher it!

If you start with **M**, your code will look like this:

Using this chart, can you break the code?
The answer is at the bottom of the page!

8 22 23 7   7 9 1 1 19 6

__ __ __ __   __ __ __ __ __ __

11 23 26 26   16 19

__ __ __ __   __ __

17 26 15 11 - 7 3 1 19!

__ __ __ __ - __ __ __ __ !

M	1
N	2
O	3
P	4
Q	5
R	6
S	7
T	8
U	9
V	10
W	11
X	12
Y	13
Z	14
A	15
B	16
C	17
D	18
E	19
F	20
G	21
H	22
I	23
J	24
K	25
L	26

GHOUL GOALS

If you want to be freaky-fly when school is back in session, set some scarylicious summer goals for yourself!

It's important for a zombie to keep her brain in top form. And what better way to do that than to keep up with pop culture?

BOOKS TO READ:

_____

_____

_____

MOVIES TO WATCH:

_____

_____

_____

Songs to learn all the lyrics to:

_____

_____

_____

Staying in shape is a scary good time, and it's good for your fins and scales too. Keep count of how much hexercise you're getting! (Use a pencil so you can easily update.)

Swimming: _____ laps

Jumping rope: _____ jumps

DANCING TO KILLER MUSIC: _____ songs

Write in your own favorite activity: _____
_____
_____
_____
_____

How much of your activity will you do this
scarecation?: _____
_____
_____
_____

Summer is a great time to beautify the world around you. You could start a compost heap; grow your own aloe plant (in case you get a sunburn!); start recycling paper, cans, and bottles; or try a beautification idea of your own.

What beautification project will you work on this summer?

_____

_____

Where will your **project** be? (Your house? Your yard? Your neighborhood?)

_____

_____

Name some **GHOULFRIENDS** who can help you out.

_____

_____

Get your petals in a row by setting up an action plan.

STEP ONE: GATHERING SCARY SUPPLIES

What will you need to get the most monstrous effect?

_____   _____
_____   _____
_____   _____

Which adults can help you with your project?

_____

_____

_____

STEP TWO: MAKING A DEADULE

Will you work on your beautification a few hours a week? Will you do it all at once? Make a plan here.

_____

_____

_____

_____

_____

STEP THREE: *Vine-centive*

You'll deserve a vine-tacular prize after you do all this work! What will you reward yourself with? A trip to the Maul? An ice scream cone?

_____

_____

_____

What other terrorific goals do you want
to set for the *summer*?

_____

_____

_____

_____

_____

_____

_____

_____

_____

_____

_____

_____

_____

_____

_____

_____

_____

GHOUL
GOALS

WILD WORDS

Circle all the words that describe what your summer will be like!

GHOULAMOROUS

beachy Cultured

AMPED UP

FREAKY FUN

scary-cute

FILL IN THE BLANKS in this freaktacular story about your amazing summer scarecation!

This **SUMMER**, I am going to do some **FANGTASTIC** activities, like _____,

_____, and _____.

I want to wear lots of ghoulamorous clothes, like

Draculaura's _____, Robecca's _____

_____, and Skelita's _____

_____. I'll visit my favorite stores at the *Maul*,

_____ and _____

_____, to pick out my killer new clothes.

One of the **BEAST** things about summer is hitting the waves. When I go swimming with the other *freshies*, I'll bring _____

_____ and

_____ with me.

I don't want to get sunburned! I'll listen to

summer scarecation songs like "_____

_____" and

"_____

_____," and I'll definitely go see the

summer BLOCKBEASTER _____

_____.

I'm going on a trip to _____

_____. It'll be **VOLTAGIOUS**!

While I'm there, I'll probably see _____

_____ and _____, and I hope

I'll get to EAT _____ and

_____ *Scarylicious*!

The one thing I'll have to take with me no matter

where I go is _____.

This $Scarecation$ will be the best ever. Just

like Frankie always says, " _____

_____

_____ "

Some other things I'll do this **summer** are:

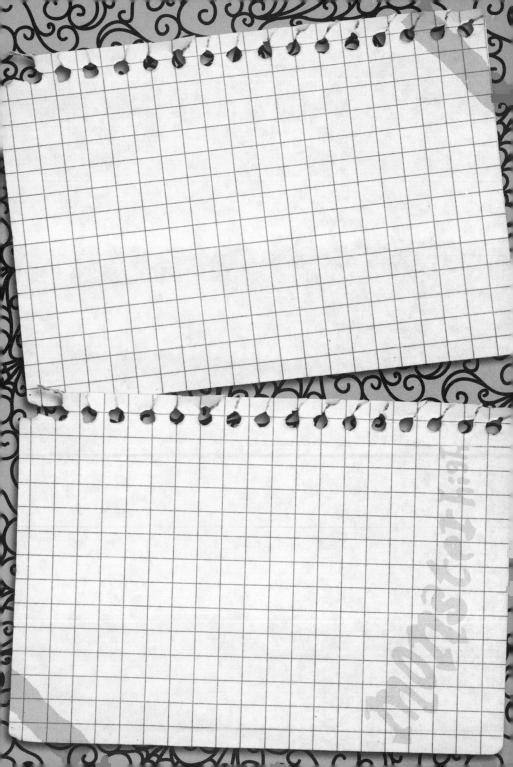

WEREWOLFICATION DESTINATION

Summer scarecation

isn't complete without a ghoulamorous vacation! For a high-quality trip, you'd better dress to impress, have the most fun you can have—and be prepared for a full moon!

Where in the world are you going this summer? Scaris, Hexico, or maybe Los Ghostas? Write all about it here!

Will you be traveling by car, plane, boat, train, or batwing?

_____

_____

_____

_____

_____

_____

However you travel, you'll need to bring some ENTERTAINMENT —
plus extra hair gel so your fur doesn't frizz en route! What activities can
you take with you?

_____

_____

_____

_____

_____

_____

_____

_____

wild
thing

Vacations are claw-some, but some things, like airplane food, are just not. What three things about your vacation are you looking forward to least?

_____

_____

_____

_____

_____

_____

_____

What **THREE** things are you looking forward to most?

_____

_____

_____

_____

_____

_____

_____

_____

_____

Planet-friendly

travel is the best kind of travel, if
you ask me. Wherever you go, you'll
want to keep the oxygen fresh and
the plants green.

Vinelicious Travel Tips

 Unplug unnecessary appliances, like the TV and
microwave, before you leave home. They use
electricity even when they aren't on!

 Instead of buying travel-size toiletries, fill small
reusable containers with the products you'll
need to stay ghoulamorous.

 Bring a reusable water bottle with you. Whether
you're a plant or not, you need lots of fluid!

 If you're staying in a hotel, ask if you can reuse
your sheets and towels, unless you've really
gotten your roots dirty.

Wherever you're staying, remember to turn off the lights when you leave a room, just like at home.

 If you go somewhere that has brochures or maps, only take as many as you need.

 Don't pick any flowers or take any other wildlife out of its environment. Instead, take a picture—it'll last longer!

Killer Style is a Must

CHEWLIAN can't always come with me when I travel. I like to bring his picture, so I don't miss him as much. It reminds me of how cute he is when he's trying to bite off someone's finger!

Which friends, pets, or family members will you miss while you're traveling? Using tape or glue, attach photos or mementos of them here.

SURVIVING FAMILY TIME

ON THE ROAD, in a hotel, at the beach— you're going to be spending some time with your family. This can be a fangtastic chance to bond, but you'll also want time to yourself. How else will you daydream about all the scary-cool boys you're going to meet on scarecation? You need a plan. And some of the ghouls have tips for ways you can make it out alive!

Draculaura

Deadphones are key, and I mean **KEY**. Put in your favorite opry tunes and drown everyone out! My favorite songs are "Blue Suede Boos" and "Greased Frightnin'." What are your favorites?

_____
_____
_____
_____
_____
_____

Operetta

Abbey

Pick up a book if you want snowbody talking to you. My favorites are **Little House on the Glacier** and **The Wizard of Ice**. What are some favorite books of yours?

_____
_____
_____
_____
_____
_____
_____
_____
_____
_____
_____
_____
_____
_____
_____
_____
_____
_____
_____
_____
_____
_____
_____

When it comes to dealing with a pack of relatives, I'm the QUEEN. The best way to keep the claws from coming out is to avoid fighting with your siblings.

 Divide all snacks evenly, or someone is gonna bare their teeth.

 No matter how tempting it is, don't invade someone else's space. It's just easier not to make the fur start flying!

 Say *please* and *thank you* — even though they're just your brothers and sisters and you may not think they deserve it!

And you know what?

If someone in your family does something totally revolting while you're on scarecation, don't keep all that anger inside. Instead, write a letter to your ghoulfriend about it. Then it'll be much easier to forgive-and forget.

Write your letters here:

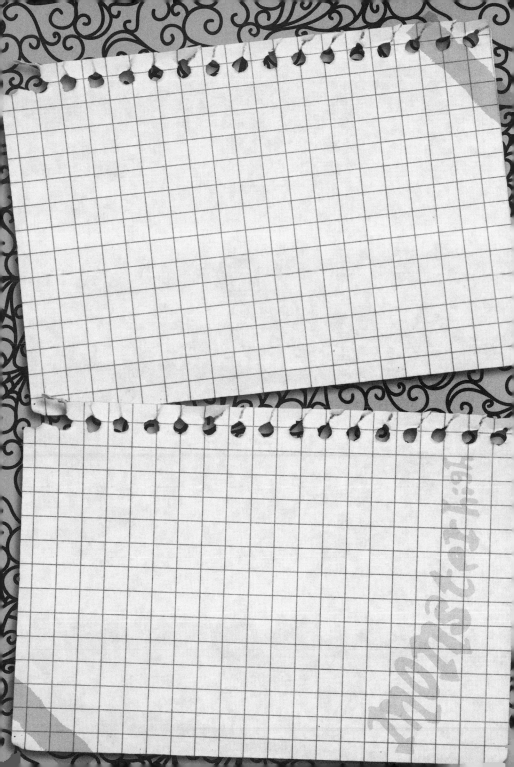

EVERYSCARE YOU GO

According to

paragraph 8.12 of the Gargoyle Code of Ethics, it is a gargoyle's responsibility to ensure travelers are prepared for their journeys. Make a list of travel essentials that you will need no matter where you go, and then check that list several times to make sure you haven't missed anything.

GargLALA

TOILETRIES

From skin scare to dental hygiene and claws to fur, taking care of your body should be a top priority! Start with this list and add your own items.

- toothpaste
- toothbrush
- dental floss
- facial cleanser
- body soap
- shampoo
- conditioner
- nail file

Socks and Underscare

Very important! Bring one clean pair for every day you'll be on vacation, plus three extras.

MONSTERTAINMENT

It is **IMPORTANT** that you bring some solid monstertainment, or you may become bored. Bring some of the items on this list and add your own.

- mp3 player
- iCoffin
- books and magazines
- Scarevel games

- snacks
- paper
- pens, pencils, or crayons
- your school's Fearbook

SET YOUR PLANS IN STONE

As a gargoyle, it is my job to warn you about the importance of planning ahead. No matter where you go on vacation, you should think carefully about what you will pack, what you will do while you are there, and all the different ways you can have some rock-solid fun. If you are prepared, you will have a très good time.

You will find suggestions here to help you pack—I cannot emphasize enough how important **sunscream** is—and ideas for ghoulamorous fashion, scarylicious snacks, and super solid games and activities, all perfect for traveling.

ROCHELLE

ROAD RAGING

Road trips can be very exciting. Par exemple, you can drive through new states, listen to rock music, and read lots of amusing signs. But road safety is not a joke, so remember to follow these rules.

- 💀 Let the driver concentrate. If there's bad weather or a lot of traffic, you may need to be quiet, or you could end up in a rocky situation.

- 💀 Keep your snacks and games where you can easily reach them.

- 💀 And, of course, use the ghouls' room every time you make a stop!

A road trip with your family offers opportunities for reading, eating ghoulicious fast food, and more reading. But you can liven up the ride if you bring the right supplies.

Packing List:

- 💀 travel pillow and blanket
- 💀 easy-to-access backpack
- 💀 Scarevel games
- 💀 deadphones and mp3 player
- 💀 sketchbook and colored pencils
- 💀 granola bars, string cheese, and crackers
- 💀 stylish slip-on shoes
- 💀 fangtastic lightweight goes-with-everything sweater

- 💀 _____
- 💀 _____
- 💀 _____
- 💀 _____
- 💀 _____
- 💀 _____
- 💀 _____
- 💀 _____
- 💀 _____
- 💀 _____

$$\Sigma(k) = mh^2 \sqrt{}$$

GHOULIA'S GAMES

Keep your brain busy with some terrorific games. It will help make the time fly.

GICK-GACK-GHOST
Hexes or ghosts? Play against a friend or sibling—or yourself.

ZOMBIE-RIFIC WORD SEARCH

To rev up the language center of your brain, find all the
Monster High words on this list. (It looks like the guys all
decided to show up too!) You can find words up, down, across,
diagonally, and backwards!

Capital
Casketball
CLAWD
Claw-some
CY
Deuce
FEARLEADING

Flashion
Ghoulgeous
GIL
GOLDEN
HEXICO
Holt

iCoffin
Jackson
Moe
MONSTERS
SCARIS
SPHINX
VOLTAGE

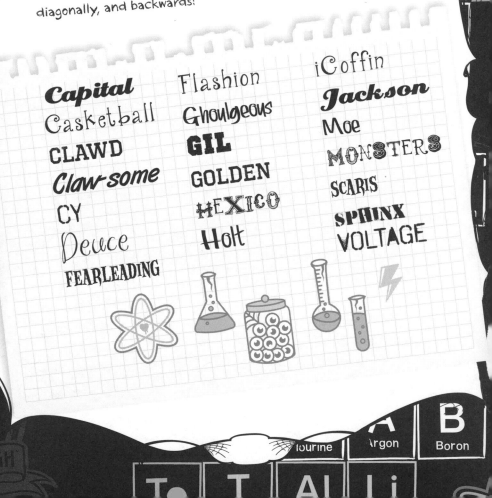

A	D	O	C	I	X	E	H	J	Z	G	R	P	Z	U
G	M	M	T	L	O	H	Y	C	S	C	A	R	I	S
G	X	L	L	A	B	T	E	K	S	A	C	M	T	P
J	B	Z	G	N	I	D	A	E	L	R	A	E	F	C
M	K	G	D	I	K	W	N	N	S	X	N	W	N	N
M	Y	A	W	R	T	O	E	U	J	L	H	I	O	J
O	V	Q	A	G	S	D	O	Y	J	Z	F	I	E	J
N	B	C	L	K	L	E	M	X	L	F	H	E	G	J
S	Y	K	C	O	G	D	D	A	O	S	M	I	A	U
T	O	A	G	L	E	E	T	C	A	O	X	Z	T	N
E	J	U	U	U	U	I	I	L	S	G	F	N	L	G
R	O	O	D	C	P	J	F	W	E	P	I	H	O	G
S	H	T	E	A	J	A	A	E	O	R	H	L	O	D
G	D	G	C	G	J	L	C	T	M	P	V	Y	V	S
R	I	A	R	E	C	X	N	I	H	P	S	F	V	Y

Answers can be found on the last page of this book.

SNACK ATTACK

To keep your fin up while you're on the road, pack some nibbles! Try this fishy recipe!

Sea Monster Surprise

You'll need:

- ★ 18 ounces cheddar cheese fish-shaped crackers
- ★ 1 ounce ranch dressing mix
- ★ 3 teaspoons dill weed
- ★ ½ teaspoon garlic powder
- ★ ½ teaspoon lemon-pepper seasoning
- ★ ¼ teaspoon cayenne pepper
- ★ ⅓ cup vegetable oil

Instructions:

1. With the help of an adult, preheat the oven to 250°F.
2. Place crackers in a large bowl.
3. In a separate bowl, combine the remaining ingredients into a seasoning mix.
4. Drizzle the mix over the crackers and toss to coat evenly.
5. Transfer the seasoned crackers to a large baking pan.

6. With the help of an adult, bake in the oven for about 15-20 minutes, stirring occasionally.
7. Cool completely and store in an airtight container.

GHOULAMOUR ON THE GO

BARE-BONES TRAVEL STYLE

When you're on the road, you have to make a little fashion go a long way! Bring along these *bonita* accessories to brighten your travel look.

- **LIGHTWEIGHT SHAWL OR SUMMER SCARF**—Wrap around your shoulders in the air-conditioned car. Turn into a belt when you hit the rest stop.

- **OVERSIZE SHADES**—Sizzle up your sockets in the sun by wearing chic oversize shades. Indoors, they double as a headband! Plastic is best; metal will get caught in your hair, and *dios mio*, that can hurt!

- **BLACK SHORTS**—The ultimate in versatility. These can be casual for a day in the park, but add a cute top and they are ghoulamorous for an upscale dinner.

Skelita

SPLIT POLTERNALITY

Game time in the car will help you avoid being dead bored. Try making up your own monster personalities!

One at a time, players make the **GHOULIEST** face they can—and make up a funny name and voice to go with it. Using your new face and voice, tell a story about your new persona! Talk about who your new character is— Sea monster? Werewolf?—and about a time when your character was in danger, won something, or learned something new. How does it end? Everyone will be dying to find out!

ghouls RULE

**READY FOR ANOTHER FANGTASTIC
GAME FOR THE WHOLE FAMILY? TRY PLANNING
THIS GHOULISH PICNIC TOGETHER!**

ALPHAFRIGHT PICNIC

The goal of Alphafright Picnic is to make a list from A to Z of all the things you're going to bring to a picnic. In alphabetical order, each player adds an item to the list. Every player has to list each item that is being brought.

HERE'S A HEXAMPLE:

- 💀 Ghoul One: "I'm going on a picnic, and I'm bringing an alligator."
- 💀 Ghoul Two: "I'm going on a picnic, and I'm bringing an alligator and a bat."
- 💀 Ghoul Three: "I'm going on a picnic, and I'm bringing an alligator, a bat, and a coffin."
- 💀 Ghoul Four has to come up with a word that starts with the letter D. Then, name all the items, including the new one.

A few more ghouls of the game:

- 💀 Once everyone has added a word, it's Ghoul One's turn again.
- 💀 Keep playing in the same order all the way through Z.
- 💀 If you can't come up with a word for your letter, you're out and the game is over!

MONSTER HIGH

FREAKY FABULOUS just got

MONSTER HIGH

CREEPERIFIC CAMPING IN THE WOODS

Nature is naturally ghoulgeous, so if you get to go camping in the woods this summer, you're scary lucky. There will be all kinds of things to do, like hiking, bird-watching, and eating s'monsters. And, of course, taking care of the plant and animal life around you!

CREEPERIFIC CAMPING PLANNING

What three plantastic camping activities will you do?

1. _____

2. _____

3. _____

CREEPERIFIC CAMPING

Spending time in nature will help you get in touch with the environment. You'll need to pack things you can do outside. And make sure your iCoffin is fully charged before you leave!

Packing List:

- tent
- sleeping bag and pillow
- flashlight and batteries
- solar charger for your iCoffin
- bug spray
- whistle
- hand sanitizer

- sketchbook and colored pencils for drawing pretty scary sightings
- nuts, dried fruit, and granola bars
- water in reusable bottles
- scary-cute hiking boots

GHOULAMOUR ON THE GO

Fabulous Fur, Claw Care, and MONSTER STYLE

Whatever you do, don't forget to take care of your fur, or it will take care of you! When you're in the woods, you can try a couple of different things.

TAILSIDE

1. Gather your hair on one side of your head, a little below your ear.

2. Leave out one strand of hair from the bottom.

3. Secure your hair with a rubber band. Don't be afraid to let it look a little messy!

4. Now that you've formed the tail, wrap the loose strand around the elastic to cover it.

5. Tuck the end of the loose strand into the tail.

Freaky chic!

SINGLE SNAKE

1. Pull your hair into a low tail at the back of your head, leaving some hair loose around your face.

2. Tease the hair in the tail by running a comb back and forth along the hair.

3. Keeping the hair in the front separate, remove the elastic from the tail.

4. Separate the hair in the tail into three sections, and braid them together very loosely.

TOO GHOUL FOR SCHOOL!

WILD CLAWS

CLAW CARE is important too, so blend in with the wildlife with some leopard print. You'll need a clear top coat, beige and teal nail polish, and a black nail art pen.

1. Paint your nails beige.

2. When the beige layer is completely dry, dot on some teal blobs—four to seven per nail. They don't need to be even or symmetrical!

3. Wait for the teal layer to dry completely too. Then, very carefully, partially outline each teal blob with black.

4. Once your nails have finished drying, add the shiny top coat.

NOW YOU'RE A REAL WILD CHILD!

MONSTER STYLE

Fashionista that you are, you know you need to look *scary-cute* while you're camping. Jean shorts, camo tops, and chic hiking boots are the way to go. Draw your most ghoulamorous camping outfit on the next two pages! Of course, your fierce fashion will need to be a perfect monster match for hiking, dealing with nature's creepy-crawlies, and getting your claws dirty.

BE YOURSELF BE UNIQUE BE A MONSTER

SNACK ATTACK

It is **very important** to keep your energy up while you're inhaling all that fresh oxygen, and the best way to do that is with healthy snacks. This recipe was passed down from troll to troll, so it's a guaranteed scarylicious feast.

Troll Mix

You'll need:

- ½ cup unsalted cashews
- ½ cup unsalted almonds
- ¼ cup dried cranberries
- ¼ cup dried cherries
- ¼ cup semisweet chocolate chips

Instructions:

1. Pour all the ingredients into a medium-size bowl.
2. Stir together with a large spoon.
3. Store in an airtight container.
4. To snack on the go, transfer a few handfuls to a sandwich bag.

INSPECTRA YOUR SURROUNDINGS

It is your duty to report on your findings in the woods, so make sure to take the time for a Freakishly Fabulous Scavenger Photo Hunt.

Circle each of the items that you are able to find below. If possible, take pictures so you'll have photographic evidence.

ACORN

bird

BUG

butterfly

GHOST TRACKS

ghouls' room sign

HAUNTED TREE

log cabin

MISTY MOUNTAINTOP

purple ferret

SPOOKY STREAM

squirrel

TROLL-FACED BOULDER

wildflower

Add your own freakishly fabulous finds:

_____   _____

_____   _____

_____   _____

_____   _____

The main reason for a VAMPFIRE is to tell spooky stories! Tell your own spooky story here, and don't forget to include some of the spooky story moments below!

"...but her head was only attached to her neck by the stitches!"

"...and then the bootiful girl ran off into the woods alone!"

"...but the tapping wasn't coming from her ghoulfriend's claws. It was coming from the roof!"

"...and the call was coming from an iCoffin...inside her house!"

NOW WRITE
YOUR STORY...

SPOOKY STORY MOMENTS

It was a dark and stormy night, and

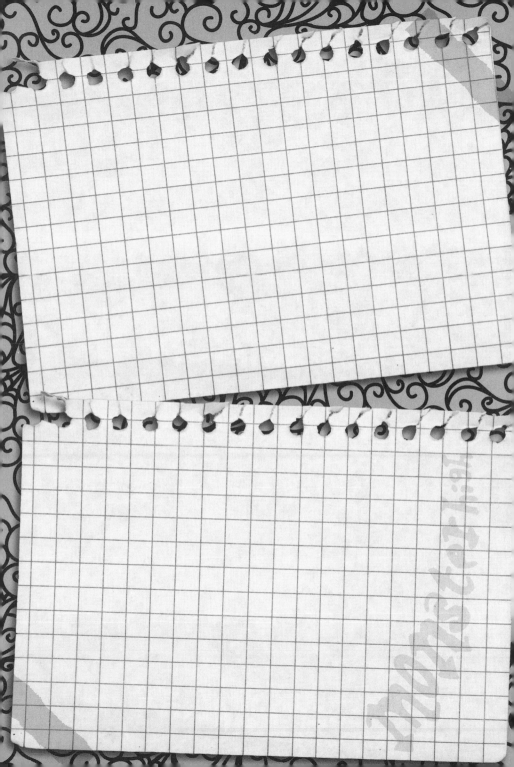

SCAREAWAY CAMP

Scareaway camp is very EXCITING! There are so many new activities in camp life for you to report to your family and friends. You'll be meeting new people, making crafts, playing sports, and having all kinds of spooky fun. Be sure to take lots of pictures and keep notes on what you're doing so you can gossip about it later.

SCAREAWAY CAMP PLANNING

What three activities are you looking forward to most?

1. _____
_____
_____

2. _____
_____
_____

3. _____
_____

Stitched Together WITH Style

At scareaway camp, you'll be the new girl—but so will everyone else! Voltage! All you need to do to fit in is bring the right stuff. You'll be sleeping away from home for a week or more, so pack enough to last for the whole time you're at camp. And bring some killer outfits, of course.

PACKING LIST:

- freaky chic sheets, blanket, and pillow
- stylish sleepwear—hel-lo, eye mask!
- pictures of your family and friends
- scarylicious snacks to share
- books, magazines, and music
- stationery, pens, addresses, and stamps

_____
_____
_____
_____
_____
_____
_____
_____
_____
_____
_____
_____
_____

SNACK ATTACK

I don't know about y'all, but sometimes I have a
hankerin' for somethin' that's both sweet and
salty. A perfect snack to bring to camp with
you will satisfy both of those cravings. And just
might help you make some new friends!

Salty Bones

You'll need:
- ⭐ 2 cups vanilla yogurt
- ⭐ 5 cups confectioners' sugar
- ⭐ 1 bag of pretzel rods (long, old-fashioned ones are best)

Instructions:
1. With an adult's help, preheat the oven to 250°F.
2. Make the frosting by combining the sugar into the yogurt one cup at a time with a hand blender in a large mixing bowl.
3. Using tongs or chopsticks, dip the pretzels into the frosting one at a time and place them on a wire cooling rack. Make sure to place a cookie sheet under the rack to catch the extra dip.
4. Once all the pretzels are coated, turn off the oven and put in the wire rack and cookie sheet, leaving the oven door slightly open.
5. Allow the frosting to harden for 3 to 4 hours.
6. After they've cooled, they're ready to eat! You can store your salty bones in an airtight container for up to three days.

The best part: They double as drumsticks!

Safety first, ghouls!

According to paragraph 18.6 of the Gargoyle Code of Ethics, it is of the utmost importance to listen to your camp counselors so that you can stay safe. Be on time for camp activities, keep your cabin clean...and have a rocking good time!

MONSTER HIGH

GET FIRED UP!

GUIDE TO GETTING INSPIRED

Whether you are making a lanyard or a sculpture or writing a play or a letter, there are many ways to light your creative fires. Try letting your thoughts take flight with some of these tricks!

Story ideas: Make your mind a blank sheet of rice paper and see what pops into it. Write the ideas here.

_____

_____

_____

_____

_____

_____

_____

_____

_____

_____

_____

_____

_____

_____

_____

ART IDEAS: Look at fashion spreads in magazines for colors, shapes, and patterns. What do they make you think of? Cut out the images that inspire you (make sure you have permission first!) and glue them here.

fashion ideas: Search for new possibilities in the world around you. Go to the garden, the kitchen, or the Maul. What fashion possibilities did you find?

MASTER WUKONG says that "all errors are opportunities." Go back to ideas you've tried that didn't work out the way you'd hoped. Use your failed ideas as inspirations for new ideas. List them below.

_____

_____

_____

_____

_____

_____

_____

_____

_____

_____

_____

_____

Jinafire

GHOULAMOUR ON THE GO

Nails in Stitches

Amp up your nail routine with some voltage stitches! You'll need a clear top coat, a black nail art pen, and nail polish that isn't too dark. Mint green is super sparky, but white or pink are good choices too!

Love The Way You're Put Together

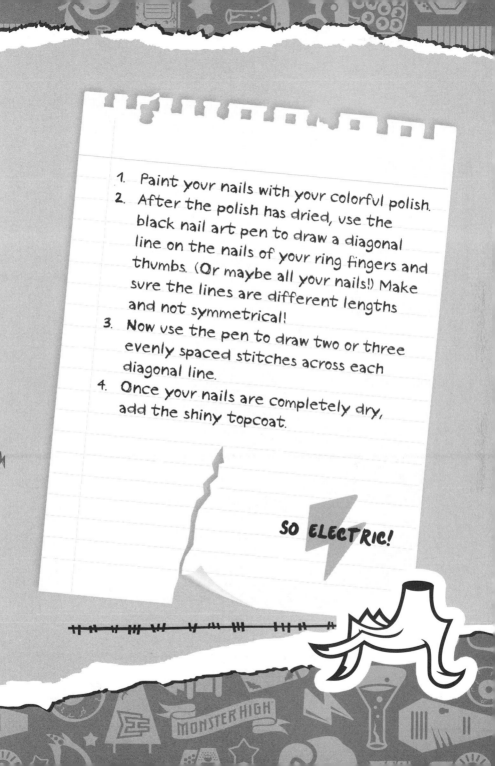

1. Paint your nails with your colorful polish.
2. After the polish has dried, use the black nail art pen to draw a diagonal line on the nails of your ring fingers and thumbs. (Or maybe all your nails!) Make sure the lines are different lengths and not symmetrical!
3. Now use the pen to draw two or three evenly spaced stitches across each diagonal line.
4. Once your nails are completely dry, add the shiny topcoat.

SO ELECTRIC!

MONSTER HIGH

TOUGH AS SCALES

One of the beast things about camp is all the batletic activities that are available. Casketball, Fearleading, swimming—they all make your gills flutter with excitement! If you want to play your best, you need to give your fins a good workout. Here are some hexercises to keep you in seafaring shape!

Octostretch

1. Stand straight with your arms stretched over your head. Reach as high as you can for eight slow counts.

2. Slowly curl your spine down until you're touching your toes. Reach as low as you can for eight slow counts.

3. Slowly curl your spine back up. Spread your legs to the width of your shoulders.

4. Lift your arms over your head, stretch them up, and then bend from the waist to your right, still facing ahead. Reach as far to the right as you can for eight slow counts.

5. Slowly bend back up to the center, with your arms still lifted over your head.

6. Stretch your arms up, and then bend from the waist to your left, still facing ahead. Reach as far to the left as you can for eight slow counts.

7. Slowly bend back up to the center.

8. Gently shake out your arms and legs.

Clam Crunches

1. Lie on your back.
2. Bend your knees, then pull them up so your thighs are perpendicular to your torso. Now cross your legs at the ankles. Your feet should be dangling above the floor.
3. Using your stomach muscles, pull your upper body toward your knees and exhale.
4. Release your upper body, inhaling as you lie back down, knees still bent.
5. Repeat ten times, then take a break.
6. Do three more sets of ten, taking a break between each set.

Seal Jacks

A seal jack is almost the same as a jumping jack, but instead of clapping your hands over your head, clap them in front of you—like a seal. How many jumps can you do in a row?

KEEPING A CAPITAL JOURNAL

Sometimes new places, PEOPLE, and routines can get a ghoul all steamed up. Keep your rivets in place and your metal oiled by writing regularly to yourself about all the robotastic activities you're doing at camp, not to mention the friends you're meeting and the capital outfits you're wearing. Time can slip away faster than a cog rolling downhill, so don't forget to write!

_____

_____

_____

_____

_____

_____

_____

_____

_____

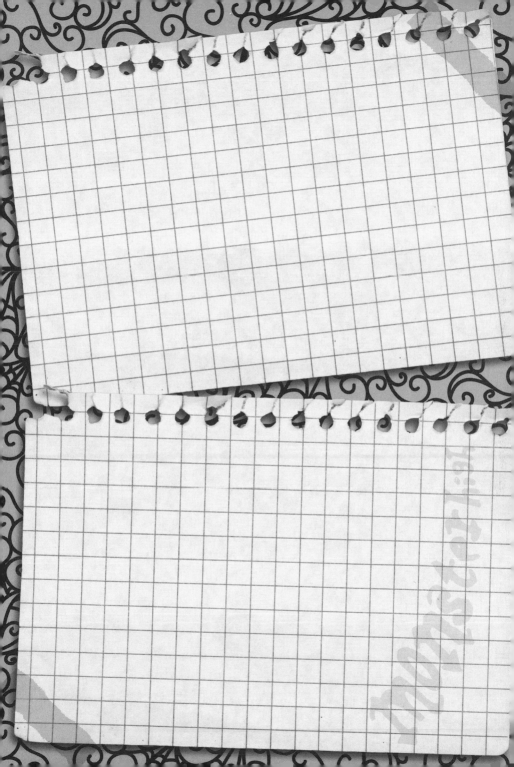

GLOOM BEACH

Going to **GLOOM BEACH** is the best way to spend the summer, gillfriend. The sun will be sizzling hot, and reflections from the water and the sand will make it even hotter, so take care of those scales by applying sunscream regularly. And some advice from Down Unda: *Stay hydrated!*

Gloom Beach Planning

What are three frightfully fabulous things you want to do at the beach?

1. _____

_____

2. _____

_____

3. _____

_____

LAgooNa

If you're going to the beach, mate, you'll need to be ready for a fintastic time! Pack your screechbag with all the sandy basics, and remember to bring lots of water—if you're a freshie, you can't drink the seawater!

PACKING LIST:

- swimsuit
- scary-cute broad-brimmed hat
- freaky fly shades
- sunscream
- towel
- terrorific beach read or magazine
- frisbee
- sand bucket and shovel
- cooler with fresh fruit and water

- _____
- _____
- _____
- _____
- _____
- _____
- _____
- _____
- _____
- _____
- _____
- _____
- _____

Keeping **COLD** is best way to enjoy heat. Important to ice up, so you do not lose your cool.

Tips on Keeping Cold

- Bring cooler full of ice. Stick face inside if necessary.

- Wear broad-brimmed hat. Stylish like a fox. Keeps sun off face.

- Rent beach umbrella. Shape is similar to igloo. Makes you cool. When you need break from sun, hang like bat under umbrella.

- Eat ice scream, Popsicle, fresh fruit. All are cool and sweet.

SO Cool

BEAST BOOKS

You should always bring something to read with you, and an old favorite is just as good as something new. My favorite books are *Pride and Poltergeist, A Zombie Grows in Beastlyn*, and *Maniac Monstergee*—and of course I like to read *Dead Fast* comic books. What are your favorite books and comics?

_____

_____

_____

_____

_____

_____

_____

_____

_____

_____

_____

_____

_____

SNACK ATTACK

You need to keep your *energy* up when you're at Gloom Beach because there is so much to do. Try this scarylicious snack when you need a boost. It is healthy, and the fruit colors are fangtastic and romantic.

Fruit of the Gloom

You'll need:
- ⭐ 1 cup grapes
- ⭐ 1 cup pineapple, cubed*
- ⭐ 1 cup watermelon, cubed*
- ⭐ Wooden skewers

Instructions:

1. Slide one watermelon cube, one grape, and one pineapple cube onto each toothpick.
2. Carefully pack the skewers of fruit into a flat container.
3. Keep in a cooler filled with ice until ready to eat.

*If the pineapple and watermelon aren't already cubed, cut them into one-inch cubes with help from an adult.

LAGOONA BLUE'S TEST OF FALSE OR TRUE

The more you know about the beach, the more fin you can have while you're here. Get a scaleful of these questions, and decide whether they're false or true. Answers are at the bottom of the page!

1. My father is the Sea Monster. **FALSE** **TRUE**

2. The ocean covers 71 percent of the earth's surface. Salty heaven! **FALSE** **TRUE**

3. Pearls get that ghostly shimmer from being made by a grain of sand inside a clam's shell. **FALSE** **TRUE**

4. Fearleading Camp takes place at North Gloom Beach. **FALSE** **TRUE**

5. The ocean contains nearly twenty million tons of gold. So ghoulamorous! **FALSE** **TRUE**

6. The average depth of the ocean is about eighty feet— much deeper than the Monster High catacombs. **FALSE** **TRUE**

1. False! And my mother is a water nymph. 2. True! It makes up 71 percent of the earth's water. Freshies aren't quite as lucky. 3. True! Either way, they look finbastic with my skin tone! 4. False! Fearleading Camp takes place at South Gloom Beach. 5. True! But most of the gold is dissolved into pieces so tiny that you can't see them. (Don't tell Cleo; she'll be disappointed!) 6. False! The average depth of the ocean is about two-and-a-half miles. Much, much deeper than the Monster High catacombs!

GHOULAMOUR ON THE GO

Skin Scare Safety Tips for Sunny Days

Skin scare is incredibly important. Your skin covers your whole body—and you want it to be healthy and soft—so you have to take extra precautions when you go to Gloom Beach.

SKIN SCARE TIPS

- 💀 Midday sun is the hottest, so be extra vigilant between ten AM and four PM.

- 💀 Apply sunscream to dry skin and allow thirty minutes for it to soak in before you go outside.

- 💀 Reapply your sunscream every ninety minutes. You can still get a totally golden tan, even with sunscream on.

- 💀 Remember your lips! Use a lip balm with an SPF.

- 💀 Salt water dries out most monsters' skin, so rinse off in the beach shower when you leave the ocean. You want to visit the desert; you don't want your skin to be the desert.

- 💀 When you're done for the day, apply a moisturizer all over to keep your skin royally smooth!

GHOULAMOUR ON THE GO

Looking like a Sphinx in the Sand

Just because you're at the beach, there is no reason to look less than absolutely golden. Every hair must be in place if you want to be a Beach Queen.

Cleo De Nile

DRESSED FOR SUMMER MUMMIN'

Beach beasties have to be fashionable, of course. You'll need to bring the perfect suit—or better yet, *two*. You'll need stylish sandals, and don't forget a monsterific summery skirt and top to wear on the way there and back. And *only* wear oversize accessories for the beach, ghouls. Anything too small might get lost in the sand.

Perfectly IMPERFECT

ROYAL LIPS

Not just **any**one can have perfectly glossed lips. To get yours, use a shimmery lip gloss in a peach or pink shade. Try to find one with moisturizer, SPF, or both.

DROP DEAD GORGEOUS

DYNASTIC 'DO

1. Sneak some tiny, snakelike braids into your hair. Sssssuper chic.

2. Select one or two one-inch sections on each side of your head.

3. Braid them, and secure with very small rubber bands.

4. When you're not in the water, add a wide headband to the look if you really want to be regal.

BEACHY KEEN

SANDTASTIC NAILS are imperative. You'll need a clear top coat, black nail art pen, and turquoise and gold nail polishes.

1. Paint the bottom halves of your nails with the gold polish.

2. After that polish is dry, paint the top halves of your nails with the turquoise polish.

3. Once your nails are completely dry, use the black nail art pen to draw thick, wavy lines across the middle of your nails, completely covering the space where the two colors meet.

4. Don't worry about making the black lines even from nail to nail; it will look more beachy if it's uneven.

5. Once your nails are completely dry, add the shiny top coat.

TOTALLY.
GOLDEN.

GLOOM CASTLE

No beach trip is **COMPLETE** without a visit to a chic, vampire-friendly castle . . . made out of sand. It's almost like being in Transylvania!

Architecture Guide

1. Live on the edge of danger—you have to make drip castles near the water's edge. Pick a spot not too near and not too far.

2. Dig a "bowl" in the sand and let it fill with water, or fill a bucket with water and add some sand to it. The sand needs to be smooth, like wet mud.

3. Make a big mound of damp sand. You can add a fence around the mound if you'd like.

4. Take a handful of wet sand and rub your fingers together over the mound of sand. The wet sand will drip down, creating creepy gothic shapes.

5. Make the castle as large and intricate as you'd like.

6. Don't forget to put bats in the belfry! And maybe a nice heart in front of the door.

Frankie

FANGERNATIONAL TRAVEL

You broaden your vision when you travel internationally. You can visit my bonita home, Hexico, or there are so many other amazing places you can go. Scaris, Transylvania, Fangland—ghoulgeous places all over the globe where you can see new things, experience new cultures, and learn all about fashions you've never seen before. Increíble!

FANGERNATIONAL PLANNING

What are three scarific sites you want to see around the world?

_____

_____

_____

Where are three places you've been?

_____

_____

_____

Where are three places you want to go?

_____

_____

_____

If you are traveling fangernationally, you need to look your beast! You also need to bring some specialty items with you. And don't forget to keep an eye out for romance!

Packing List:

- 💀 passport (so you can get through creepstoms)
- 💀 power outlet adapters (to keep your iCoffin charged)
- 💀 translation book or app (to speak the fanguage)
- 💀 guidebook (to provide details on monster history)
- 💀 _____
- 💀 _____
- 💀 _____
- 💀 _____
- 💀 _____
- 💀 _____

Flashion List:

- 💀 chic scarf, perfume, smelly cheese (Scaris)
- 💀 bat wings, black cape, garlic (Transylvania)
- 💀 scary-cute bathing suit, sunscream, salsa (Hexico)
- 💀 _____
- 💀 _____
- 💀 _____
- 💀 _____
- 💀 _____
- 💀 _____

ROMAN HOWLIDAY

One of the beast parts of **FANGERNATIONAL** travel is planning your ideal scarecation. If you could go absolutely anyscare and do absolutely anything while you were there, what would you do? Write all about it here!

Clawdeen

GARGOYLES ON A PLANE

Traveling **internationally** can be complex. Mark off the items on this list and be prepared.

- Make sure your water bottle is empty before you go through security. You can fill it up at a water fountain once you're through the gate.

- Be ready to take off your shoes and jewelry before going through the metal detector. Hope your claws are polished!

- Have your passport ready when you get to customs.

- Keep your luggage with you at all times.

IN-FRIGHT ENTERTAINMENT

 Listen closely to all safety instructions at the beginning of and during your flight.

 Pack the latest must-read novel on your list. You may be able to finish it!

Bring a book of logic puzzles, corpsewords, or boodoku.

 Bring a notebook for writing spooky stories or sketching monsterpieces.

 Look through the in-fright magazine. Rank the items for sale on a silliness scale of 1 (for least silly) to 5 (for most silly).

 Don't fight with your siblings! Remember that other passengers are on the plane with you.

Pack some yummy, healthy snacks. Also pack gum to chew during takeoff and landing to keep your ears from popping.

Study a beginner's guide to the language of the country you're visiting. Nothing is more Scarisian than understanding *un petit peu de français*.

SPEAKING THE FANGUAGE

Before you head overseas, you need to learn some KEY PHRASES in the fanguage of the country you're visiting. Using a language book or the Internet, find the translations for these phrases and write them in so you have easy access to them.

Hello!

_____

_____

_____

HOW ARE YOU?

_____

_____

_____

WHAT IS YOUR NAME?

_____

_____

My name is _____

_____

_____

_____

It's nice to meet you.

_____

_____

_____

How much does that cost?

_____

_____

_____

WHERE IS THE BATHROOM?

_____

_____

_____

I'm looking for my family.

_____

_____

_____

WINGSPIRATION

Traveling to a **NEW COUNTRY** can give you so much wingspiration! There are new foods, new fashions, and new buildings. Depending on where you go, the social customs are different. You should closely observe the behavior of the locals and try to imitate it, so that you do not accidentally offend anyone.

LOCAL CLAWTURE

Some **CLAW-SOME** places to visit in a new place are bootiful museums, the locations of important historical events, and local markets. Write down some places that you will visit on your trip.

_____

_____

_____

_____

_____

_____

_____

_____

_____

_____

_____

_____

_____

_____

_____

FANGERNATIONAL FASHION

One of the **BEAST** things you can do when enjoying another country is buy a fashion magazine to see what the local ghouls are wearing! Their clothes and accessories may not be available where you live, but you can use the magazines to come up with new and exciting fashion ideas. Go through the magazine and cut out the most bitetastic pieces. Tape or glue them here to inspire your future wardrobe.

PRETTY *in* PINK
BUT BETTER *in* BLACK

SCALE MAIL

If you *visit* another country, least you can do for your ghoulfriends is send them postcard. Make postcard extraspecial by personalizing. Bring stickers and markers with you. Buy postcard of bootiful local scenery and add your own touches. You will need to buy local airmail stamp. Then drop in mail!

Draw your own postcard design for the country you are visiting:

DEAD BORED

Summer scarecation

is full of fun, but sometimes it seems like there is nothing to do. It's horror-ble! But don't let boredom give you the boos. Nothing is sparkier than trying out things you've never done before, so when you are at bats' end, try some of these killer activities. They'll turn monster bleak into monster chic!

GHOULENTEER

Score some **KARMIC** savings by ghoulenteering for your family and neighbors! Earn flowers to become a higher level Ghoulenteer.

Each time you do anything on the ghoulenteer list, you earn flowers!

- 🌸 carrying in the groceries = **1 FLOWER**
- 🌸 washing a car = **1 FLOWER**
- 🌸 taking out the trash = **1 FLOWER**
- 🌸 keeping plants' skin shiny and green by helping out with a lawn or garden = **2 FLOWERS**
- 🌸 walking a pet (such as a dog, bat, or dragon) = **2 FLOWERS**

Try to reach Ghoulenempress before summer ends!

12 flowers: Junior Ghoulenteer
16 flowers: Ghoulenteer
20 flowers: Senior Ghoulenteer
24 flowers: Ghoulenprincess
28 flowers: Ghoulenqueen
32 flowers: Ghoulenempress

Monster High

Track your **FLOWERS** with this chart!

GROCERIES	car	TRASH	plants	PET

STREET MAUL

G*H*OUL, you need to get into the entrepreneurial spirit! To raise some cash, try starting a business in your neighborhood. There are all kinds of claw-some companies you could start!

- organize a scarage sale
- have a carwash
- raise money for scarity
- sell spooky snacks

What are some of your own summer **BUSINESS** ideas?

_____
_____
_____
_____
_____
_____
_____
_____
_____
_____
_____
_____
_____
_____
_____
_____
_____
_____
_____
_____
_____
_____

BLUEPRINTS OF THE NEIGHBORHOOD

Get to know the **ARCHITECTURE** in your neighborhood, yard, or even apartment really, really well by drawing a monster map. Take careful notes on where all the streets, houses, bushes, hideouts, and rooms are. Include all the details that you can. For extra ghoulishness, add gravestones in the most creative places possible—and don't forget to add in some gargoyles, *bien sûr.* Gargoyles give buildings special protection from evil spirits.

SLINGING CABLES

VAMPING is totally voltage! But if you want to keep in shape for Fearleading, bring a jump-rope cable with you, and try these moves!

KEEP IT! TOGETHER!
FRANKIE

Maybe you know this one already.

Basic Cable

1. Hold one end of the cable in each hand, with the cable hanging behind you.

2. Swing the cable forward over your head, and jump over it.

3. Keep going! See how many jumps you can do in a row.

4. Now add a cheer to the rhythm of your jumping:

M-O-N-S-T-E-R-S.
MONSTERS, MONSTERS,
YES, WE ARE!

CROSSED CABLE

1. Hold one end of the cable in each hand, with the cable hanging behind you.

2. As you swing the cable forward over your head to jump over it, cross your arms in front of you.

3. After you jump, bring your arms back to their original position.

4. Once you get the hang of it, you can count your jumps and add the cheer.

how bout you?

One-Legged Crossed Cable

Sometimes you cheer so hard that you lose a leg over it! Don't let that stop you, though. This jump is the same as Crossed Cables...but on one foot! Bend your other leg at the knee slightly so that it isn't touching the ground. Again, once you've mastered this, you can count your jumps and add in the cheer.

STUDY ANCIENT HISTORY

Get activity ideas from the **GHOSTS OF SUMMERS PAST**! Ancient times were pretty spooky, so talk to three different adults about their favorite summer activities from when they were young monsters. Write them here and then try them!

Spectra

Ghost of Summers Past #1

Ghost name:

_____
_____
_____
_____
_____

How do you know this ghost?

_____
_____
_____
_____

What ideas did this ghost give you?

_____
_____
_____
_____

Ghost of Summers Past #2

Ghost name:

_____

_____

_____

_____

_____

How do you know this ghost?

_____

_____

_____

_____

_____

What ideas did this ghost give you?

_____

_____

_____

_____

_____

Ghost of Summers Past #3

Ghost name:

_____

_____

_____

_____

_____

_____

How do you know this ghost?

_____

_____

_____

_____

_____

What ideas did this ghost give you?

_____

_____

_____

_____

_____

INDOOR FREAKTIVITIES

What's a ghoul supposed to do when it's RAINING bats and frogs? Take the party inside, that's what! But don't just watch TV, play video games, and text your ghoulfriends on your iCoffin. Instead, get your body moving. Otherwise, you might contract a case of the rainy-day boos.

List some fun indoor activities you like to do.

_____

_____

_____

_____

_____

_____

_____

ROCK THE CAPER

STRUTTING your stuff under the fright lights and singing your heart out while your fans howl your name? Well, now, what ghoul wouldn't want to be a rock star? And the first thing a rock star has to do is pick a band name.

Circle one of these howlarious names, or come up with your own!

THE FAB FUR
Simone & Gargoyle
LED ZOMBELIN
THE VAMPETTES
Howl City

Write your name here: _____

Band name picked? Rockin'!
Now pick a scarylicious song title!

Circle one of these spooktacular titles, or write your own!

"MATERIAL GHOUL"
"It Had to Be Boo"
"Starfright"
"I Fought the Claw"
"FANGNAM STYLE"

Write your titles here: "_____"
"_____"
"_____"
"_____"
"_____"

And now it's time for the lyrics.

Here are some quick tips. Each verse is different, and each line of the verse is different. Try making the first two lines rhyme with each other, and the second two lines rhyme with each other. The chorus is the same every time. Try making the first, second, and fourth lines the same, and the third line different.

HERE'S AN EXAMPLE TO GET YOU STARTED:

Verse:

It's time to sing a monster song.
You know the words, so sing along.
Wave your hands up in the air,
Dancing like you just don't care.

CHORUS:

It's a monster party.
It's a monster party.
It's time to get wild.
It's a monster party.

Now write some lyrics of your own!

Verse:

_____

_____

_____

CHORUS:

_____

_____

_____

Verse:

_____

_____

_____

CHORUS:

_____

_____

_____

_____

Practice your song with whatever melody you want. You can use one you know (like the melody to "Twinkle, Twinkle, Little Star") or you can make up your own as you go.

Now put on your most fangtastic outfit and perform your claw-some new tune for your family, your pets...or your stuffed zombiphant!

HOWLSEKEEPING

In a big family, it's a ghoul's RESPONSIBILITY to help the howlse stay in good shape. And you can always turn your work into a dance party with wild music and a lot of energy! The more bows you earn, the more iCoffins you get to decorate.

Each time you do anything on the howlsekeeping list, you earn bows!

- dusting = 1 bow
- emptying the dishwasher = 1 bow
- watering plants = 1 bow
- feeding pets (like cats, snakes, or owls) = 1 bow
- folding and putting away the laundry = 2 bows
- cleaning your room = 4 bows

12 bows: iCoffin 1   24 bows: iCoffin 4

16 bows: iCoffin 2   28 bows: iCoffin 5

20 bows: iCoffin 3   32 bows: iCoffin 6

Track your *bows* with this chart!

DUSTING	dishes	plants	PETS	LAUNDRY	ROOM

Try to decorate all the iCoffins before summer ends!

FEARLEADING DANCE

A Fearleading dance has to wow. It has to amaze. It has to make the audience say, "Oh my rah!" Are you up to the challenge of choreographing your own ghoulish dance routine for the Dance of the Delightfully Dead? Good. Let's go, ghouls!

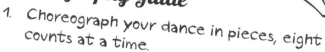

Choreography Guide

1. Choreograph your dance in pieces, eight counts at a time.

2. Pick a golden song with a good beat.

3. Start out with an eye-catching Egyptian pose.

4. Get the crowd's attention by not doing anything for the first eight counts. (The counts are the beats of the music.)

5. At the beginning of your dance, use simpler moves, like "step together, step touch." Get more complicated as you go, and bring out the big leaps and turns in the grand finale.

6. Strike a big pose right before the music ends. Stay in position and listen to all that applause!

7. Take a big bow. You've earned it!

Don't forget to put together the perfect costume before you perform. Something fun. Something sparkly. Something with tights underneath!

SCARY STORIES WITH GHOULIA

A story could have many different endings. This story has a beginning, but the end is up to you. Write about the ghoul and her favorite things. Include a few of her friends and family members. Then show what terrorific event happened to her over the summer and how she handled it.

Once upon a time, there was a ghoul with deadly charm. It was her summer scarecation, and she...

Ghoulia

Just because this story is finished doesn't mean you have to stop! You could write a story with different characters but the same first line. Or you could even write a different story about the same characters!

FRANKENVENTIONS WITH FRANKIE

Some of the **SPARKIEST** new stuff is made from recycled parts! You can get freaky chic clothes at a thrift store and update them with your own touch. You can use an empty soda bottle to grow a houseplant. You can even stitch your old T-shirts into a creeperific quilted blanket.

What other things could you make out of recycled parts? Write down your wildest ideas—like turning kites and tights into working bat wings! What other Frankenventions could you make?

_____

_____

_____

_____

_____

_____

_____

_____

_____

_____

Now list some **IDEAS** you can actually try—without having access to a scientific laboratory, that is.

_____
_____
_____
_____
_____
_____
_____
_____
_____
_____
_____
_____
_____
_____

Try making some of your Frankenventions come to life!

YOUR GHOULFRIENDS ARE WITH YOU IN SPIRIT

Even if you *don't* see your ghoulfriends every day, they're the beast friends you have. Would one of your friends make a good ghost or zombie? Do you have a friend who would look claw-some with fangs, wings, and violet skin? Let your creative fires burn and draw them all here!

PETRIFIED

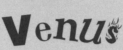

Venus

Pets **FEAR** you up when you're feeling down and help you stay envined with nature. So why not get a new pet? Make one for yourself and for each of your friends!

You'll need:
- construction paper
- scissors
- glue
- pencil
- markers
- 1 foot of thin ribbon
- glitter (optional)
- sequins (optional)

Instructions:

1. Using pencil on construction paper, draw an animal no larger than a quarter of a page. Start with a simple shape, like a cat or frog, and then add fangs, horns, wings, or other monster parts.

2. Cut out the animal.

3. Decorate it with markers. You can add glitter and sequins too. Now think of a name for your new pet!

4. Cut out a rectangular piece of construction paper that is a little more than twice as large as your pet. Carefully fold the paper in half, like a card. Your pet will go inside the card.

5. Using markers—and glitter and sequins if you want—decorate the front of the card with your pet's name.

6. Glue the ribbon horizontally across the back of the card, and set it aside.

7. Cut a lengthwise strip of construction paper. Make it a little thinner than your animal.

8. Make a fan: From the end, fold an inch of the paper forward to touch the strip. Holding this together, fold an inch backward, and so on until the end.

9. Glue one end of the fan to your pet and set a heavy book on it to help it stay in place while it dries.

10. After it's dry, glue the other end of the fan to the inside of the card (where a message would usually be printed). With the card open flat, place the fan in pre-springing position. Again, set the book on your pet to help it stay in place while it dries.

11. Once this is dry, close the card and tie the ribbon around it in a bow.

When you or your friends untie the ribbon and open the card, your pet will spring out at you!

THE END IS NEAR

Watch all of your clocks, **GHOULS**! Scarecation is winding down, and there are a few things you should strap into your schedule before it's over. You won't be able to face yourself if you don't get your cogs' worth out of summer—you can count on that!

RobeCCa

Visit a **SCREAM PARK**! If you haven't gone to one yet this summer—well, even if you have—take this chance to ride some scary-fast ghouler coasters and squeal louder than the wheels of a freight train.

SCREAM PARK TIPS

- 💀 For shorter lines and steam-free skin, go on a cloudy day. (But not a rainy one!)
- 💀 Don't forget your fashion! Wear some riveting closed-toe shoes, a cute denim skirt, and a lightweight top. Plus some oversize jewelry, of course!
- 💀 If the park will let you leave for lunch, pack one in a cooler for a relaxing picnic.
- 💀 When the line for your favorite ride is short, go again and again!
- 💀 Always, always, always buckle up.

SNACK ATTACK

Summer is the best time for ice scream. It's also the best time for brain freeze. And scareberries. This is making me hungry. Try this recipe!

Scareberry Shortcake

You'll need:
- 1 scoop vanilla ice scream (per serving)
- 1 angel food cake
- 1 container whipped scream
- 1 pint blueberries
- 1 pint strawberries

Instructions:

1. Rinse the blueberries and strawberries.
2. With an adult's help, hull and chop the strawberries. Set aside.
3. With an adult's help, cut the angel food cake into individual servings.
4. Put one scoop of ice scream on each angel food cake serving.
5. Add whipped scream.

6. Sprinkle a handful of blueberries and a handful of strawberries on top.

YUM!!!

HAZY DAISY CHAINS

Make a **SPIRITED** fashion statement with flowered jewelry fit for a summer monster. You can make chains for yourself, and you can make them for all your cousins and friends too. You can wear them as necklaces, bracelets, and even crowns. Qué linda!

Making Hazy Daisy Chains

1. Find a patch of daisies, and make sure you're allowed to pick them. (You can also buy daisies or use another flower, like clovers.)

2. Pick several daisies.

3. Take one daisy, and using your thumbnail, put a half-inch slit near the bottom of the stem.

4. Now take a second daisy, and slide its stem through the slit. Now they're linked!

5. Keep repeating the previous two steps until you've reached your desired length.

6. To close off the chain, make a one-inch slit in your final daisy, instead of a half-inch slit.

7. Put the head of your original daisy through this slit. (Remove the petals if necessary.)

8. Wear your daisies with pride!

GO FIN DEEP

You're stoked to see your *mates* every day when school starts, but you'll miss getting your flippers wet once the weather cools down. So take one last dip in a freshwater monster's foyer while you still can!

Swimming Tips

- 💀 Now's the time to show off all the laps you've done this summer. Break out any cool tricks you've learned while you're at it!

- 💀 Bring a beach ball to the pool for some water volleyball, water polo, or that old standby, catch.

- 💀 Remember to wear sunscream and drink plenty of water. But not pool water! Not even freshies like to drink chlorine.

SHOP UNTIL YOU DROP DEAD

For totally claw-some back-to-school fashion, make one last trip to your favorite store! Try these fashion tips!

- Mix this season's full-price items with sale items and thrift-store finds for a totally hair-raising outfit.

- Shop around! Browse several stores before picking out what you just have to have.

- Accessories can change a whole outfit! Cardigans, jean jackets, scarves, headbands, and chunky jewelry are perfect for fall.

BATTY BACK-TO-SCHOOL FUN

SCARECATION IN REVIEW

What fiery trips and **fangtastic** fun did you get into this summer? Whether you traveled abroad, went to Gloom Beach, had a vamping adventure, or went to scareaway camp, you did new things and met new people. One of the best parts of summer is remembering how fun it was. If you write it down now, it can inspire you later.

Where did you go on **VACATION**? What did you do there?

_____

_____

_____

_____

_____

_____

_____

_____

Did you meet new *ghoulfriends*? What do you like about them?

_____

_____

_____

_____

_____

_____

_____

_____

_____

_____

_____

What was the most claw-some outfit your wore?

What was the MOST TERRORIFIC thing you did?

What was the **LEAST TERRORIFIC** thing you did?

What did you not do that you want to do **NEXT** summer?

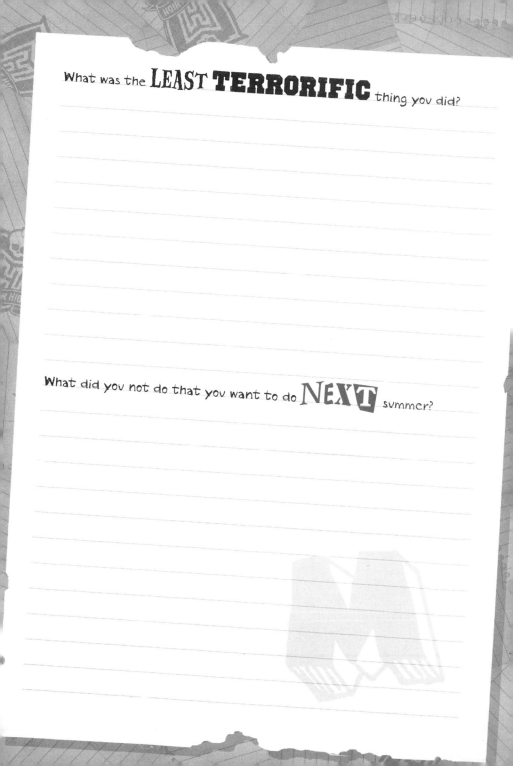

PHAROAH PHASHION

Making a first **IMPRESSION** is always important.
Just ask the Sphinx. *Nobody* forgets about her, do they?
To make sure you're a big hit, design your ghoulamorous
first-day-of-school outfit—mummy wrappings and
armbands included—and make certain it's freaky chic!

Back to school means back to snacks! It is important for a growing vampire to eat a variety of delicious nibbles. Here's a list of yummy monster snacks to put in your lunchbox!

- ☐ cashews
- ☐ fish-shaped crackers
- ☐ string cheese
- ☐ gummy bears
- ☐ grapes
- ☐ chocolate chip cookies
- ☐ dried cranberries
- ☐ _____
- ☐ _____
- ☐ _____
- ☐ _____
- ☐ _____

- ☐ _____
- ☐ _____
- ☐ _____
- ☐ _____
- ☐ _____
- ☐ _____
- ☐ _____
- ☐ _____
- ☐ _____
- ☐ _____

DEADULE

Keeping up with your **SCHEDULE** in the new school year is as important as keeping your boiler full. You'll need some capital school supplies to make sure you can keep track of your classes and schoolwork!

- 💀 daily planner
- 💀 pencil case
- 💀 pencils and pens
- 💀 erasers
- 💀 binders
- 💀 loose-leaf paper

- 💀 _____
- 💀 _____
- 💀 _____
- 💀 _____
- 💀 _____
- 💀 _____
- 💀 _____
- 💀 _____
- 💀 _____
- 💀 _____
- 💀 _____
- 💀 _____
- 💀 _____

Toralei

PASS THE MONSTER

Scarecation may be over, but the fun never stops. Get in the mood for Deaducation by playing a back-to-school game with your ghoulfriends!

Instructions:

1. All ghouls stand in a circle.

2. Ghoul A turns to the ghoul on her right (Ghoul B) and makes a monster noise with a monster face.

3. Ghoul B passes the noise and face to Ghoul C, who passes it to Ghoul D, and so on.

4. Keep passing the monster from one ghoul to another, around and around the circle.

5. Even though you'll try to match the noise and face exactly, it will gradually change into a new monster noise and face.

6. Add in hoof and claw movements—shake your fur! Whisper and howl! Go wild!

FITTING IN IS SO OUT!

SO SPOOKTACULAR!

SUMMER SCARECATION HAS COME TO AN END!

You've had a pretty **SCARY** summer, jam-packed with **vacations**, trips to the beach, all the *family* time a ghoul could need, and plenty of *ghoulamour*. Maybe you WROTE a song or story, solved a PUZZLE, or **choreographed** a dance. Just becavse scarecation is over doesn't mean the fun has to **STOP**! You can think of some BUSINESS ideas or Frankenventions for the fall, and you can write notes to your friends in UNCREEPABLE Code. So keep the FANGTASTIC times going. Have a scary school year. And stay ghoulgeous, *ghoulfriend*!

Answer to Zombie-rific Word Search.

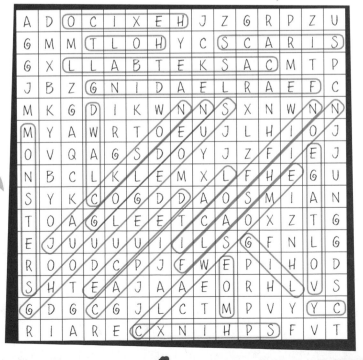

Check out the amazing series!